FIRST NIGHT

AWAY FROM HOME

by

MYRA BERRY BROWN

pictures by

DOROTHY MARINO

FRANKLIN WATTS, INC.
575 LEXINGTON AVENUE
NEW YORK 22, N.Y.

For Lorna, Betsey and Jonathan

4 5 6

Library of Congress catalog card number: 60-11014.
Printed in the U.S.A.
by Polygraphic Co. of America

FIRST NIGHT
AWAY
FROM HOME

Stevie was busy packing his suitcase.

He was invited to spend the night at David's house.

They were best friends to each other.

He was excited!

Stevie had never slept away from home before.

He packed his
> rock collection
> squirt gun
> airplane
> hair brush
> tooth brush
> tooth paste

"I have everything I need,"
   said Stevie to his mother.
"You forgot your pajamas,"
   Mother told him.
Stevie laughed.
He went to get his pajamas.

Everything just fit in the suitcase.

He snapped it shut.

"I can carry this suitcase myself," said Stevie.

He lifted it to show his mother.

Mother kissed Stevie good-by at the front door.
"Have a good time and sleep tight," she said.
"I'll see you in the morning."

Stevie started out.

David's house was the yellow one
  at the end of the block.

Stevie could see David standing
  in front and waving at him.

Stevie felt very grown-up.

Stevie walked past Cindy's house.
Cindy was roller-skating in front.
"I'm on my way to spend the night
    at David's," Stevie said.
"Have you ever slept away from home?"

Cindy slowed down.

"Oh yes!" Cindy said.

"Last summer I even slept in a hotel.

I heard lots of trucks on the highway.

It was fun."

Stevie came to the twins' house.

The suitcase was getting heavy. Stevie changed hands.

Peter and Paul were riding in their wagon.

"I'm going to spend the night at David's,"
  said Stevie.

"Have you ever slept away from home?"

Peter said, "We slept in the hospital one whole night."

Paul said, "We had our operation."

"We got presents," said Paul.

"We got sore throats," said Peter.

Stevie passed Kathy's house.

Kathy was getting on her bike.

"I'm going to spend the night at David's house,"
  Stevie told her.

"Have you ever slept away from home?"

Kathy said,
   "I sleep at my grandmother's all the time.
   My grandfather snores."

Stevie came to little Bobby's house.

Stevie thought Bobby was probably
 too little to understand.

Bobby was pushing his tractor.

"Where are you going?" Bobby asked.

"To sleep at David's house," Stevie told him.

"I never sleep away from my house,"
said Bobby.
"I sleep with my Teddy Bear."

Just then David ran up to meet Stevie.
"Hi," he said. "Come on in."

David's room had bunk beds.
"You can sleep on top if you want,"
   said David.
Stevie opened his suitcase.
He took out his airplane.
He sailed it up high.

It landed on the top bunk bed.
Stevie climbed up the side ladder to get it.
"I'll sleep up here," he said.

After dinner, David's father said,
"Stevie is your guest, David.
He should choose the book tonight."
Stevie chose *The Horn that Stopped the Band.*

Stevie and David got ready for bed.
Stevie took out his pajamas and
   tooth brush and tooth paste.
He let David try his tooth paste.
"It tastes better than mine," said David.
David's mother called in,
"Your beds are ready, boys."

David's room looked different at night.

Stevie climbed up and got in bed.

It did not feel like his bed at home.

David's mother turned out the light.

"Good night, boys," she said. "Quiet down
now, so you can fall asleep."

David giggled.

It sounded funny to Stevie up on top.

He giggled, too.

Pretty soon Stevie looked down at David.
David was already fast asleep.

Stevie turned to one side.
Stevie turned to the other side.
He could not fall asleep.

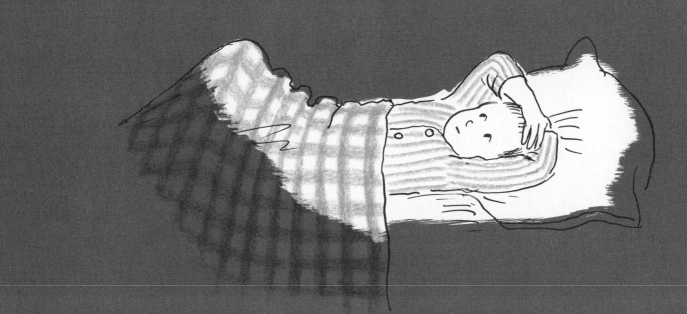

He watched the ceiling.
He watched the wall.
But nothing helped him sleep at all.

TRUCK

SNORE

Then he heard the front doorbell.
He could hear someone talking softly.
Stevie sat up.
Soon David's mother tiptoed in.
"Stevie," she whispered, "I have something for you.
Your mother sent it over.
You forgot to pack it."

She handed Stevie his Teddy Bear.

Stevie smiled.

He could feel his bear's smooth button-eyes.

He felt the soft end of his nose.

He hugged the Teddy Bear tight.

And then Stevie fell fast asleep.